Land Pirates

vs.

Sea Ninjas

A Brief History

Written and
Illustrated by

Grae Hunter

Dedicated to my Folks -
Thanks for letting me not grow up.

ISBN: 1466202785
ISBN-13: 978-1466202788

Land Pirates
vs.
Sea Ninjas

Have you ever wondered where and how Landboats were invented? How Ninjas can walk on water?

Or just wondered what would happen if Pirates and Ninjas had a fight?

Now you can find out how it all began, How Pirates created a need for Sea Ninjas, and how those same Sea Ninjas created Land Pirates.

Now you can know it all.

Written and Illustrated by

O.
Gnae Hunter

In the year 1369AD the Pirate problem off the coast of Japan had become a major issue. Emperor Chokei tried sending his Samurai to deal with the pirates. The honorable Samurai were ill prepared for sneaky, deceitful pirates.

If the Pirates thought they might lose a battle they would request 'Parlay' to negotiate a time & place to fight, – Then being pirates they just wouldn't show up.

China.

JAPAN

Pirates

it has been ... ...at Pirates
are naughty ... ...esn't make
it true.
Many pirat... ...aughty but
recent scie... ...en choose a
some crisis... ...to the life
of Piracy...

Reason:
if there ... ...be this,
and when ... ...ave,
had ab... ...and
lets f...
it, t...

Emperor Chokei had heard that you should fight fire with fire, and though two villages had already been burnt and lost to this technique, he thought it might apply better here, by employing sneaky Ninjas to fight sneaky Pirates.

Initial engagements had indeed proven better. However after 6 months, the Ninja's' weapons had become rusted. The Pirates more accustomed to the sea water and supply requirements, enjoyed their only period of real victory over the Ninjas.

Unwilling to accept defeat, or pay for new weapons constantly, the Ninjas started to utilise the resources of the sea itself. So throwing stars, katana and nunchakus became starfish, swordfish and octopus to name but a few. These new weapons had many benefits:

1 These weapons never rusted, and in the event they did become damaged they could easily be replaced, without the need to return to shore

2 After a battle they could eat their weapons to restore energy.

Sea Ninja Weapons

Sea Ninjas have a variety of weapons available to them. [...] just a little [...] the service of the [...]

figure 2.f

octopus	Octopus
	Fish Fish
	Flounder Fish
	Clam Shell
	Star Fish
	Sword Fish

The pr[...] [...] sticky creatures like [...]

The[...] [...] the Pirates, but also [...] the fish into fresh [...]

The idea that you could list every weapon a sea [...] [...]egorize all the creatures in the ocean, be it Gia[...] [...]lly fish nets all the poison strands knotted in [...]

If its nasty, the Sea Ninja will use[...]

figure 2.g

Techniques

figure 3.a

The fish slap:

Striking with the fish in either back or fore hand.

Often the key to the fish slap is aimed at the face.

[...]urfing:

[...]res of the sea, sharks made a [...] with the Sea Ninjas to help fight the Pirates if the Sea Ninjas would help them fight pollution.

Strapping the seaweed rope as a bitten bridle allows the shark to remove the bridle at its pleasure.

figure 3.b

Not returning to port, meant the Ninjas could sail indefinitely and it is at this point, in 1467, that the split between the traditional Ninja guild and the new Sea Ninja guild occurred. These new Sea Ninjas quickly became the terror of the high seas, for Pirates and Privateers alike.

Often Sea Ninja vessels would appear to be abandoned ships, but once the Pirates had boarded, they would discover 50 Sea Ninjas were hiding on deck. After a while the Pirates stopped boarding what they now called "Ghost Ships".

Sea Ninja Creed

All Ninja that life on the sea m̄ ... ...̄ever more be chained to the nearest piece of lana ... ...aptured in the high sea where the nearest land is t̄ ...

1. You must equip yourself with in ... ...from the Ocean

2. Piracy is to be slapped in the face ā ... ...r fish, octopus. Whatever is at hand.

3. Thought shall not sl̄ ...

4. Honour the master all̄ ... ...l confusion.

... ...while eating.

... Ninja and remember the 318 step code of confusion. ... remember.

The Sea Ninjas however, started tying flounder to their feet with seaweed so they could walk on water. This meant by the time the Pirates got close enough to realise that it was a ghost ship, they had come too close and now had 50 Ninjas on the deck of their ship. Which was quickly followed by a face full of fish.

Sea Ninjas would often start a fight by throwing sticky creatures like starfish and octopus at the Pirates to slow them down and then fish would be used to slap them about a little. For nearly 300 years Sea Ninjas slapped Pirates with fish and fish like sea life.

The only escape was to beach their ship and retreat in land, as the Sea Ninjas had sworn never to set foot on land again.

This didn't work well for the Pirates that beached themselves in Japan or Sam 'Snail Wit' Rogers who retreated up river, and found being slapped by otters and eels just as bad as fish.

The Pirates had in their defence, invented plungers in 1812 to remove octopus and starfish, and many Pirates replaced their hooks with these new plungers.

Plunger Patent

For use by Pirates and pirate affiliated business only
Anyone found to be reproducing plungers or sticky sea
removers as they were initially know by, will bring about
a war of pir-epic ptopotions. Trust me those are big

It's hard to say wat the inner workings of the device
were meant to be, but the only real thing you need
to concern yourself with is the rubber bit, and that goes
to key bit

In 1836 Red Beard the rude sat on the shores of the Americas wallowing in sadness, full-grown Pirates openly weeping at his side. A merchant happened by in his wagon, and foolishly thought he might make a quick sale on handkerchiefs.

When Red Beard the rude saw the treasure chest on wheels roll up, he had a revolutionary idea. The merchant of course had a feeling of unease caused by Red Beard's growing grin, and rightfully so. Red Beard ordered his crew to capture the wagon and take its wheels. Then adding them to the beached long boat, he fashioned a sail from the wagon's cover.

Red Beard had created the first land boat and fathered the concept of Land Piracy.

The Tale of
Red Beard the Rude

...Land Pirates who don't know the name
...h Rude. Famous not only for the
...im the name, but also for allowing
... land as at sea.

...d that first discovered that
... attached to a long boat
... and in a way sail.

Fish Slapped

... ttering

most ...

Beached to Escape Sea Ninjas

The Way of The Land Pirate

There are some amongst you that would doubt even the existence of land pirates. Let along believe that the live by a strict… well strictish code. This code allows Pirates to share territory without t...

It basically breaks down to 12 codes of which any one pirate is allowed ... uld a Land Pira... ... ll in the possesion of more than 8 of the codes, ... ssesion of only 4.

This ba... ... be gained when ... ... ame t hat will e...

The... ... ... we...

... allowed to know up to

... himself in the possesion

... until he is in possesion

... re to be gained when

15.

They made the merchant and his horse walk the plank. This was not as deadly as it had been in shark infested waters, and instead they chose a particularly prickly bush. The merchant was happy to survive the encounter, and considers himself doubly lucky as the bush was covered in berries, and he was quite hungry from the ordeal.

8.

It didn't take long for other Pirates to follow suit, and though the initial land boats weren't very manoeuvrable and firing a cannon could flip a small vessel, it was still considerd better than fighting Sea Ninjas.

THE BEGINING

The original plan with land boats was to create ambushes and swoop in on wagons, but if the Pirates miscalculated they would race past, then as they stopped to change direction they'd lost the element of surprise. A clever wagon driver would simply turn his wagon two or three times, losing the Pirates altogether.

Of course land Pirates had taken up a philosophy of change and adaptation. Faster and more manoeuvrable swoops were invented and it was discovered that if they fired straight up while also firing broadside, on the same side, it would prevent the boat from flipping.

They also discovered it was best to do this while moving, as the falling cannonball wouldn't sink their land boat, but it could cause havoc for their foot should it land there.

Land Boats

The Long Boat or "Dirt Bath" as it became known was the first landboat. It had notouriosly bad steering.

Life boats became often quicker and Dirt Baths, th

Some design are better than others, although quick and manuverable the triSwoop had a habit of falling over.

Modern Land Boats

Land Pirates were one of the early adopters of the motor vechile, and the big convertables were actually designed by Land Pirates of the time.

Some Modern Land Pirates still hold to the old ways and have been known to attach cannon or even planks and crows nests to larger cars or Land Boats if you will.

These were not the only changes for the Land Pirates. The traditional parrots had had their wings clipped to prevent them from flying away, and though they were poor swimmers they were excellent walkers and hoppers.

With monkeys and parrots leaving, Land Pirates found squirrels to be more applicable to their needs. Originally they had had success with raccoons, but they were just too big to sit on a Pirate's shoulder.

BOB LAND'T

ow they were on land, and not being regularly pelted with jelly and starfish, squid or octopus, they still kept the plungers. Plungers became very useful for harpooning the newly invented cars and bald people.

f course in 1954 when the plunger was patented Pirates were furious and orchestrated the Great Rubber Robbery of 1958, when they raided and stole all land-based transports and warehouses of plungers, worldwide in a single day.

o pirate has had a need for plungers since. Stories of a mountain filled with plungers are whispered about on cold nights, of course no one has ever seen it and lived, unless they were a Land Pirate captain.

Of course anyone can turn to Land Piracy, and it's almost common for accountants and parking wardens to lean towards this notorious lifestyle given the chaos and danger of their day-to-day job.

But always the Sea Ninjas wait. If you go down to the foreshore on the full moon, while the tide retreats, you might see young Land Pirates testing metal and plungers against fish and octopus, daring fate as they battle the flounder footed Sea Ninjas.

The never ending battle, of Land Pirates vs Sea Ninjas

Pirate

Yo-hu glue and my staple gun
Gonna steal all the pencils
Just for fun.

Land piracy is the life for me
Driving and laughing
Til my pants i fee.

I hate this job, I want
to be free a Pirate on
the open road.

crew

cannon

me

Colouring in Page

Feel free to photocopy this page for colouring/coloring purposes

Colouring in
Page
Feel free to photocopy this page for colouring/coloring purposes

Colouring in
Page
Feel free to photocopy this page for colouring/coloring purposes

Colouring in
Page
Feel free to photocopy this page for colouring/coloring purposes

Colouring in
Page
Feel free to photocopy this page for colouring/coloring purposes

Paper From DeviantArt.com

Coffee paper 003 by AbigelStock
Old paper HUGE 01 by Ayelie stock
Old Paper HUGE 03 by Ayelie stock
Old paper texture by haunted medea
Paper texture 5 by wojtar stock
Paper texture v5 by bashcorpo
Paper Texture 2 by Insan Stock
Paper Sheet 001 by reflected stock
File Case Cover 001 by reflected stock
Paper013 by AbigelStock
Grungy paper v 6   or sumtin   by bashcorpo
Plays 10 Records by Smoko Stock
Grungy paper texture v 12 by bashcorpo
Grunge paper texture by arghus

Paper From Bittbox.com

Grundge 01
Grundge 02
Grundge 03

Super Big Thanks

★Bartek Nowak
★Anthony Scally

Made in the USA
Lexington, KY
02 December 2012